For Henry
—A.R.

For Basil
—C.R.

Text copyright © 2016 by Adam Rex
Illustrations copyright © 2016 by Christian Robinson
A Neal Porter Book
Published by Roaring Brook Press
Roaring Brook Press is a division of Holtzbrinck Publishing Holdings Limited Partnership
175 Fifth Avenue, New York, New York 10010
The art for this book was made using acrylic paint and collage techniques.
mackids.com

Library of Congress Control Number: 2015034414

ISBN: 978-1-59643-964-1

First edition 2016
Printed in China by RR Donnelly Asia Printing Solutions Ltd., Dongguan City, Guangdong Province
1 3 5 7 9 10 8 6 4 2

SCHOOL'S FIRST DAY OF SCHOOL

story by
ADAM REX

pictures by
CHRISTIAN ROBINSON

A NEAL PORTER BOOK
ROARING BROOK PRESS
NEW YORK

That summer, they dug up the big field, and poured the foundation, and set brick on top of brick until they'd built a school.

A sign above the door read, FREDERICK DOUGLASS ELEMENTARY. "That's a good name for me," thought the school.

Most days a man named Janitor came to mop the school, and buff his floors, and wash his windows. "This is nice," the school said to Janitor. "Just the two of us."

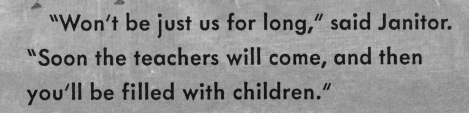

"Won't be just us for long," said Janitor.
"Soon the teachers will come, and then
you'll be filled with children."

The school creaked. "Children?"

"All *kinds* of children. They'll come to play games and to learn."

"Oh," said the school, "will you be here?"

"You'll see me after the school day is over,"
said Janitor. "Don't worry—you'll like the children."
But the school thought that Janitor was probably
wrong about that.

Then they came, the children did, and there were more
of them than the school could possibly have imagined.

They got *everywhere*. They opened and closed all of his doors and lockers, and drank water from his fountains, and played on his jungle gym. "So *that's* what that is for," thought the school.

Some of the older kids gathered by the
school's back fence and showed each other
their bored faces.

"This place stinks," said one, and
the school gasped.

"I hate school," said another with puffy
hair, to the agreement of his friends.

The school sagged a little.

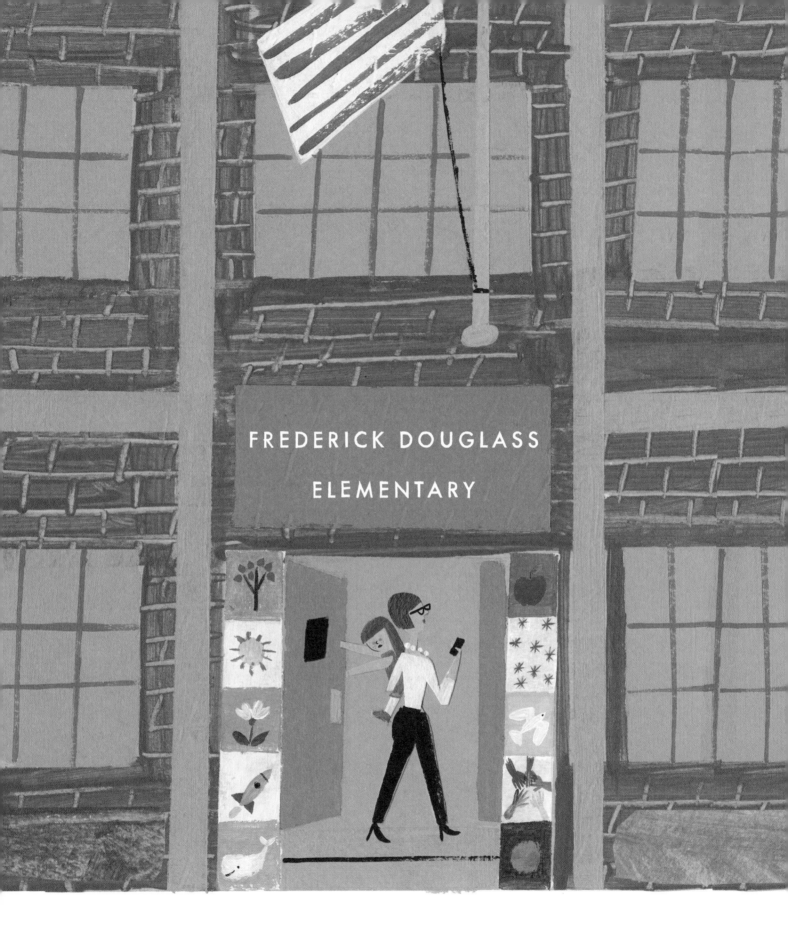

One very small girl with freckles didn't want to come
inside the school at all. Her mother had to carry her.
"I must be *awful,*" the school whispered to himself.

Later he squirted the puffy-haired kid in the face,
then felt bad about it afterward.

He watched the kindergarten kids sit on one of his rugs.
The teacher said, "As we go around the circle, please
tell us your name."
There was an

Aiden,

and a Max,

and a Bella,

The small girl with freckles was next, but she wouldn't speak. She only stared at her shoes until the teacher moved on.

"I don't like school," she whispered into her lap.

"Well . . ." thought the school, "maybe it doesn't like you either."

and a Chloe.

and a Caiden,

and an Emma,

and another Aiden,

The children were in their chairs, finally. But just as the school was starting to relax, his fire alarm sounded, and all the children exited and walked to the other side of the field and stared at him.

He was so embarrassed.

He held his doors open for them when they returned. "Sorry," he said, as the first child entered. "Sorry. Sorry. Sorry," he told them all. Even the girl with the freckles.

At twelve o'clock the school was filled with food.

At twelve thirty the school was filled with garbage.

At one table a boy told a funny joke, and another boy laughed so hard that milk came out his nose.

"Now I'm covered with nose milk," thought the school.
He had to admit that it was a pretty funny joke, though.
Even the girl with freckles liked it.

After lunch the kindergarten kids learned about shapes. "A rectangle has four sides," said the teacher. "One, two, three, four. And a square has four sides, too. In fact, a square is actually a special kind of rectangle!"

"Wow," said the school. "I did *not* know that."

Afterward the children made pictures with glitter and paste. The girl with freckles made a picture of the school. "It looks just like me," thought the school. "Except glittery. It's like she's known me all my life."

"Do you think I could have your picture?" the teacher asked her. "Don't tell anyone, but I think it's the best." The school thought she was probably right about that.

The freckled girl smiled when the teacher stuck her
drawing onto the school wall with a pushpin.
"Ouch," said the school. But he didn't mind, not really.

At three o'clock, the parents came to pick up the children.

At three thirty, Janitor came to pick up the school.

"I was full of kids," the school told him. "And I heard a joke, and I accidentally had a fire drill but everyone was nice about it, and I listened to a classroom and learned about shapes."

"You had a big day," said Janitor.

"Do you think . . ." the school said. "Do you think you could invite everyone to come back tomorrow? Especially that little freckled girl?"

Janitor nodded. "I'll see what I can do."

Later, Janitor sat on top of the school, and they watched the sun go down.

"In the beginning I didn't know what I was," said the school. "I thought I was your house."

"Nope," said Janitor.

"I . . . I suppose some *other* place gets to be your house," the school added.

Janitor nodded. "That's true. But you get to be a school. That's lucky."

And the school thought he was probably right about that.